Mr. Crumb's Secret

Phyllis J. Perry

Illustrations by Ron Lipking

WITHDRAWN

UpstartBooks

Fort Atkinson, Wisconsin

For Casey, Clare, Julia, and Emily.

Published by UpstartBooks
W5527 Highway 106
P.O. Box 800
Fort Atkinson, Wisconsin 53538-0800
1-800-448-4887

Fribble Mouse was a small gray mouse who lived in Cheddarville, Wisconsin. Two things really stood out about Fribble. He had an extraordinarily long tail, and he was extremely curious.

Fribble loved football and baseball. He was very good at science and math, although not too quick at reading in his second grade class at Twitch Elementary School. He adored eating fresh green peas, sesame crackers, sunflower seeds, and Gouda cheese. He liked visiting the zoo and the park. But most of all, he loved a mystery.

Directly across the street from Fribble lived a friendly mouse, named Mr. Crumb. Mr. Crumb lived alone and spent a lot of time working in his beautiful garden. Sometimes Fribble went over and helped.

Curious Fribble always had a million questions to ask—how, when, where, what, why—and Mr. Crumb patiently answered all of them. He even explained why grass is green, which is a very tough question! And he never seemed to grow tired of his little neighbor. When Mr. Crumb lost his trowel or couldn't find the nozzle for his hose, Fribble stopped asking questions and moved into action. He had an uncanny ability to find missing objects.

One Thursday afternoon in September, Fribble went over to Mr. Crumb's right after he got home from school. He helped Mr. Crumb in the garden and then they sat on the porch, nibbling cheese and drinking lemonade. Fribble stroked his whiskers, lounged back in his chair and gave a little squeak of contentment. Then he asked, "Don't you ever get tired of working so hard in the garden, Mr. Crumb?"

"Funny thing you should ask that," Mr. Crumb said. "As a matter of fact, I never get tired of my garden, and I miss working in it during the wintertime. So I'm thinking of taking up a new hobby. Something I can do when the snow falls and the garden is resting."

"A new hobby?" Fribble said. He quickly swallowed the bit of cheese he had in his mouth and sat up straight and alert in his chair. His nose wrinkled up and down making his whiskers wiggle the way they always did when his curiosity kicked into high gear. "What's your new hobby going to be?"

Mr. Crumb smiled. "It's a secret," he whispered.

"A secret?" Fribble repeated, lowering his voice to a whisper, too, as he softly said one of his favorite words. He put down his frosty glass of lemonade and turned all his attention on Mr. Crumb. "But what is it?"

Mr. Crumb laughed. "If I told you, it wouldn't be a secret any more, would it?"

"Fact is," he continued, "I'm going to learn to do something. At least I hope I am. I'm sure going to try very hard. You go off to school every day now that summer vacation's over and you learn things all the time. But it's been a long time since I've studied and learned something new. So I'm going to keep my new hobby a secret until I learn how to do it. Then I'll tell you all about it."

Fribble thought fast. "Maybe," he said, "if you told me about it, I could help you learn. I'm pretty good at addition and subtraction. I can read short, easy books. And I know an awful lot about caterpillars and butterflies."

"I'll remember that," Mr. Crumb said. "But I think I have to learn about my new hobby all by myself. Then I'll show you," he promised. "Or," he said, and Fribble noticed the twinkle in his eye, "maybe since you're so good at mysteries, you can discover my secret all by yourself. I challenge you to try."

Fribble gave a shudder of eager anticipation! A challenge! Since he couldn't coax this out of Mr. Crumb, he'd figure it out all by himself. He finally left to go home for dinner, but he promised himself that he would keep his eyes and ears open. He was sure he could discover the secret before Mr. Crumb told him.

Late Friday afternoon, Fribble was playing catch with his little brother, Scamper, in his front yard when the mail truck came. Instead of just putting letters in the mailbox, the mailman carefully took a parcel out of his truck and carried it right up to Mr. Crumb's door and rang the bell.

Smack! The football that Scamper threw hit Fribble right in the stomach because he wasn't watching. His eyes weren't on the ball. They were on the long, thin parcel that the mailman handed over to Mr. Crumb. Could this have something to do with the secret?

That night, just before he fell asleep, Fribble thought about the package again. What could be in it? What was long and thin? Golf clubs? Skis? A pogo stick? Tent poles? The bow for a violin? What was Mr. Crumb's secret hobby?

The question was still in Fribble's mind when he went down to breakfast the next morning. After breakfast Fribble's mother reminded him, "Don't forget it's trash day. Be sure you take the trash can out to the curb first thing."

"I will," Fribble said. He went out into the garage and wheeled the garbage can right out to the curb. Then he noticed that Mr. Crumb had already put his trash out. The lid wasn't on his can the way it usually was because a discarded, long thin box was sticking way up out of the can.

Fribble's nose began to twitch. He looked to the right, and he looked to the left.

No one was in sight. Quickly, Fribble ran from his trash can right over to Mr. Crumb's.

He stared at the box. It had a bright sticker on it, but Fribble couldn't read the words. Again he looked to the right and the left. Then he jumped right up onto the trash and, using his teeth, he tore off the part of the package containing the label.

Holding it tightly in his paw, Fribble darted back across the street and took the label up to his room. He smoothed it out on the floor and tried to read the three words.

The door opened and little Scamper came in. "What are you doing?" he asked.

"Reading," Fribble said.

"Reading what?"

"Reading this label, of course."

"What's it say?" asked Scamper.

"I'm not sure," Fribble admitted. "These words are hard."

"Ask mom," Scamper suggested.

Fribble thought for a moment. If he asked his mother, would that be cheating? Mr. Crumb had challenged him to figure out the secret by himself. It wasn't really fair to ask her. "I'm going to figure it out for myself," Fribble said. "And I don't want to wait until Monday to go to the school library. I'm going to go to the public library this morning."

"Can I come?" asked Scamper.

"Sure," Fribble agreed. "If you can remember how to act in a library," he added.

Scamper looked serious. "No running and yelling," he said. "And handle books carefully. With clean paws," he added.

"You got it," Fribble said. He folded up the label from the box and shoved it into his pocket.

He and Scamper went downstairs to find their mother. "Is it okay if we go to the library this morning?" Fribble asked.

"Of course," his mother agreed. "But be back before lunchtime."

Fribble and Scamper walked down the street. The library was only a few blocks away and they had often gone there during the summer for story hour. They both knew the librarian, Miss Scurry. They walked up the old, stone steps and right up to the desk where Miss Scurry sat. "May I help you?" she asked.

Fribble took the label out of his pocket and spread it out on the counter. "I want to look up these words," he said. "I want to know what this means."

"You need a good dictionary," Miss Scurry said. She took Scamper and Fribble over to a table in the reference area and brought a big dictionary to them. "Do you know how to use this?" she asked.

"I've looked up some words in the dictionary at school," Fribble said. "But it took me an awful long time to find them."

"Guide words will help," Miss Scurry said. "Let me show you. Your first word is 'F-R-A-G-I-L-E.' You start out by looking in the dictionary at the words that start with the letter 'F.'"

Miss Scurry helped the boys look up both words, learn how to pronounce them, and understand their meanings. But when she was finished, Fribble was discouraged. He knew how to read the two words now, fragile and antenna, and he knew what they meant, but he still didn't know what Mr. Crumb's secret was. Could it be a very delicate insect?

"Whatcha thinking about, Fribble?" Scamper asked when his brother continued to sit at the library table, staring down at the dictionary.

"Antenna has two meanings," Fribble said. He read slowly. "Feelers on the heads of insects and crustaceans and wires to send radio waves."

"I know what insects are," Scamper said proudly. "We're learning about them in kindergarten. They're bugs. But what's a crustshun? The only crusts I know are on pieces of bread."

"I don't know what they are," Fribble said, "but I know that a crust of bread doesn't have an antenna. Guess I'd better look it up and find out."

Fribble slowly worked his way through the

pages of the dictionary until he found "crustacean." "They're things like shrimps and lobsters and crabs," he announced to Scamper. He pulled the torn box label out of his pocket along with his stubby pencil and carefully wrote "insects," "crabs," "shrimps," and "lobsters" on the back.

"Oh," Scamper said, looking thoughtful. "Do you think Mr. Crumb's box had bugs in it or shrimps?"

"I don't know," Fribble said. "I think we have to find out more. And I don't think it would be cheating to learn to use the library."

The boys walked back over to the librarian's desk. "Miss Scurry," Fribble asked, "do you have any books about insects, crabs, shrimps, and lobsters?"

"Sure. Lots." Miss Scurry said. "Do you know the name of the book you're looking for?" Fribble sadly shook his head. He looked around. There must be a million books in this library. How was he ever going to find one to help him? He was beginning to think that he would never be able to solve Mr. Crumb's mystery.

But Miss Scurry didn't look sad at all. She was smiling. "You need to learn how to use our computer catalog," she said. "I'll show you."

Miss Scurry took Fribble and Scamper over to a

computer no one was using. The computer screen said "Welcome to the Cheddarville Public Library."

Miss Scurry pointed to the screen that had lots of words on it. Fribble and Scamper crowded in close on either side of her. "This is the one you want to use," she said. "It says 'Library Catalog.' It has a list of all our books."

"Wow!" Fribble said.

She clicked on it. "You can choose 'word,' 'name,' or 'title.' If you know the name of the author, click on 'name.' If you know the title, click on 'title.' Since you don't know either, click on 'word' and type in what you're trying to find. You'll get a list of books and you can pick one. Go ahead and try it." Miss Scurry got up, and Fribble sat in the computer chair.

Fribble pulled out the label with the words he'd copied from the dictionary. He typed "insects" into the box on the computer screen. He made a mistake, but Miss Scurry showed him how to correct it. Then he hit the "enter" key and up came a whole list of books.

"Here's one," Fribble said, pointing to the screen. There was a note of excitement in his voice. "It's called *All About Bugs*."

"Great!" Scamper said. "Let's go get it."

Fribble started to climb out of the chair and then stopped. "But where is it?"

Miss Scurry said, "Look at the screen again. Right after your book's name, do you see the numbers 595.7? The numbers tell you where to find the book. It's a nonfiction book. I'll show you where to start looking."

She walked over to the stacks of books, and Fribble and Scamper followed. She pointed out where the 500s section of books was.

"Is this it?" Fribble asked, pointing to a book with the number 595.672 on its spine.

"No," Miss Scurry said. "There are lots of books in the 500s section. You have to keep looking until you find 595.7." Then she left them to search on their own while she went to help a woman.

Fribble looked at the numbers on the spines of the book until he found 595.7.

"It's right in here somewhere," Fribble said to Scamper. "There it is!" he cried, and took *All About Bugs* from the shelf. He and Scamper sat down on the carpet to take a look.

"Hurrah!" Scamper said. "It has lots of pictures.

This is a great book. Let's take it home." He scrambled to his feet. Then he stopped. "What about the crusts?" he asked.

"Good thinking, Scamper," Fribble said. "I almost forgot them."

They took their bug book and walked back to the computer. Fribble clicked on "Library Catalog," and then he clicked on "word." He pulled the label out of his pocket again, and this time he typed in "crabs." Lots of titles appeared on the screen.

"Look at this one," Fribble said. "It's called *Crabs and Crustaceans*."

"Perfect," Scamper said. "It's exactly what we want!"

"Where do we look for this one?" Fribble asked. He looked for the numbers after the name of the book. This time the numbers were 595.386. "Hey," he said. "It must be close to where we were before."

Scamper and Fribble went back to the stacks of books again and soon found the one they wanted. They carried the two books over to Miss Scurry. Fribble put the books on the counter. He reached in his pocket for his library card and flipped it down on the books.

"Looks like you found just what you were looking for," Miss Scurry said with a smile. She checked out the books and handed them and the card back to Fribble.

"Can I carry one?" asked Scamper.

"Sure," Fribble agreed, and they hurried toward home, each carrying a book.

When they got to their house, they could see Mr. Crumb working in his garden across the street. "Hello," he called. "Want a glass of lemonade?"

Looking both ways, the boys crossed the street.

"We've been to the liberry," Scamper said as they ran up on Mr. Crumb's porch and sat down, "and we got two books."

"You did?" Mr. Crumb said. He hurried inside for a pitcher of lemonade and some glasses. As he poured, he asked, "And what are you reading?"

Scamper proudly held up the book he was carrying. "It's all about bugs," he said. "Fribble's book is all about 'crusts.'"

"Not 'crusts,' Scamper. It's about crustaceans," Fribble explained.

"Well, those books look interesting. Very interesting indeed," Mr. Crumb said.

"Raising insects or crustaceans might be an exciting hobby, don't you think?" asked Fribble. He carefully watched Mr. Crumb's face for any reaction.

"It might be a fine hobby," Mr. Crumb agreed.

"They have antennas," Fribble said, emphasizing the last word as he spoke.

Mr. Crumb looked surprised for a moment, and then he laughed out loud. "You're right," he said. "They do."

"If you want to borrow this book after I read it," Fribble said, "I'll let you."

"That's very nice of you," Mr. Crumb said. "But I've already checked out some books from the library myself, and right now I'm busy reading them."

"Oh," said Fribble. "What book are *you* reading?"

"This one," Mr. Crumb answered. He held up a thick book that was on the big, wooden arm of his porch chair.

"Does it have any pictures?" asked Scamper hopefully.

"No, it doesn't," Mr. Crumb said, "but it's very interesting. Now drink up your lemonade. It's almost time for lunch and you don't want to worry your mother."

As Fribble stood up to go, he paused long enough to take a quick look at the title of Mr. Crumb's book. He wasn't sure, but he thought it read "Gooey Macaroni."

Fribble and Scamper went home with their books, but Fribble was feeling more confused than ever. Gooey Macaroni? Had he read it wrong? Cheese and macaroni was one of Fribble's favorite dishes. Was Mr. Crumb planning to take up cooking for a hobby? But what did cooking have to do with "fragile" and "antenna"?

After lunch on Saturday, Fribble and Scamper lay down on the soft carpet in the living room to look at their books. They opened the insect book first. It was filled with color photographs of all kinds of fascinating bugs. The praying mantis was especially long and skinny and weird looking. And the long-horned grasshoppers had enormous antennas, which were what they were looking for.

When they looked in the book about shrimps, crabs, and lobsters, they found it was interesting, too. But intriguing as the books were, Fribble had a nagging feeling that he was on the wrong track. The long, skinny box that was delivered to Mr. Crumb was way too big to be full of insects, even the long praying mantis. And to live, the crustaceans would have to be bought at an aquarium shop and carried home in water.

The curious little mouse who usually had so much to say and so much to ask was unusually quiet. His mother finally asked, "Do you feel all right, Fribble?"

"Yeah, I'm fine," Fribble said.

"What fun things did you do at school last week?" his mother asked.

Fribble tried hard to stop thinking about Mr. Crumb's secret and to remember the highlights of last week at school. "We started something new called SSS, Share Something Special days," Fribble said.

"What are they?" asked Scamper.

"You sign up on a list if you have something extra special that you want to share with the other kids," Fribble explained. "And on your SSS day, your mom or dad or someone else who's special can come to school if they want."

"That sounds interesting," Fribble's mother said. "What sorts of things have people brought to share?"

"Snuffle's grandmother came on Wednesday, and she brought a quilt that the two of them made this summer. It had lots of little squares of cloth in it and about a zillion tiny stitches."

"What else did kids bring?" asked Scamper.

"Tweek brought his stamp collection last Monday, and on Friday, Scruffy brought a trophy that he won playing tennis."

"Cool," said Scamper. "What are you going to bring on your SSS day?"

"Don't know yet," Fribble said. "But it has to be something super special."

Fribble looked in his closet and was happy to find several things that had been missing for a long time, including his favorite blue racing car and his first baseman's mitt, but nothing extra special for SSS day. He had some good baseball cards, and he had a fine rock collection. But he'd brought them to school before.

That night for dinner, Fribble's mother served Fribble's favorite, macaroni and cheese. This started him thinking about Mr. Crumb's secret. Was the book Fribble had seen on the porch really called "Gooey Macaroni?" He wished he'd taken a longer look at the title and copied it down. What could macaroni have to do with Mr. Crumb's new hobby? Was he going to take up cooking? Or write a cookbook?

"This is great, Mom," Fribble said, taking a second helping. "Is it hard to make?"

"I'm glad you like it, Fribble. It's one of the easiest of all the pasta dishes."

"What's a pasta dish?" asked Fribble.

"Oh, things like spaghetti, lasagna, ravioli, and macaroni. They come from Italy."

"Ah," Fribble said. His nose twitched, and his mind raced. Maybe Mr. Crumb's hobby had something to do with travel. Maybe he was planning a trip to Italy and was reading up on what to eat, like gooey macaroni, while he was there.

That night as he lay in bed, Fribble thought how great it would be if Mr. Crumb traveled around the world and sent him lots of postcards with strange stamps on them. He could even take the postcards to SSS day.

In the morning, Fribble thought more about pasta dishes and Italy. Where was Italy, anyway? He decided he'd better find out. The public library didn't open until noon on Sunday, so it wasn't until after lunch that Fribble, and tagalong Scamper, headed back down the street.

"Are we going to get more books about crusts and bugs?" Scamper asked cheerfully. He loved going through books and looking at the pictures.

"No," Fribble said. "I want to look at some maps this time. I want to know where Italy is."

"Is it far away?" Scamper asked.

"Yes," Fribble said. "At least I think so."

"As far away as the farm where Grandpa and Grandma Mouse live?"

"Even farther, I think," Fribble said.

Once they got to the library, Fribble and Scamper went right up to Miss Scurry.

"Why, hello," she said and gave them a big smile. "Are you back for more books about insects and shrimps?"

"No," Fribble said. "Today I want to know about Italy."

"Italy?" Miss Scurry said. "And what exactly do you want to know?"

"Well," said Fribble, "the first thing I want to know is, where is Italy?"

"That's a good place to start," Miss Scurry agreed. "For that, let me take you to our reference area and get a big atlas for you to use."

"What's an atlas?" Fribble asked.

"It's a great big book of maps," Miss Scurry explained.

"Can we check out the atlas?" Fribble asked.

"No," Miss Scurry said. "I'm sorry, but our atlas stays here in the library. It's big and heavy and very expensive. So we keep it handy here where anyone who needs it can use it. Why don't you sit right at this table, and I'll bring an atlas to you."

Scamper and Fribble climbed up into chairs at the big library table. Scamper sat on his knees to make himself taller.

Miss Scurry brought over a big atlas.

"Is it like a dictionary?" Fribble asked. "Do you use guide words?"

"I'm glad you remembered guide words," Miss Scurry said. "But no, you use an atlas differently from a dictionary." She opened the book near the beginning. "This is a table of contents," she explained. "It's a list of everything that's in the book and what pages to look on."

Miss Scurry ran her finger down the page. "See, here in the beginning there are maps of the solar system, climate maps, and special maps about where plants and minerals can be found. Then there are maps of different parts of the world. First, let's look at a big map that shows the whole world." She looked up in the index to find the page for the world map.

She opened the book to a map that took up two pages in the book. "Right here," Miss Scurry said, "is where we live." She pointed to a part of the map. "This is the continent of North America, and this piece is the United States of America. Here's where we live in Wisconsin. Over here is the state of California. And up here is the state of New York. Here's the Atlantic Ocean," she went on. "And right across the ocean is the continent of Europe. This piece, that's sort of shaped like a boot, is the country of Italy."

"Wow!" Scamper said. "Italy is a long, long way from here."

"Yes, it is," Miss Scurry said. She turned back to the index. "Now let me find a map of Europe, and you can get a better look at Italy." She turned to the index and looked up "Italy." It referred her to page 49, G8. She opened the atlas to page 49 and showed them a big map of Europe. She put one finger on G and another on 8, bringing one finger across and one finger down the page until they met.

"I see Italy," Fribble said. He pointed to the boot-shaped country.

"That's it," Miss Scurry agreed. "Now when you've finished looking, you let me know and I'll put the atlas away." Miss Scurry left them.

Fribble stared at the big map with shining eyes. Italy was a long way off. Would Mr. Crumb be going to Italy? Would he eat lots of gooey macaroni? Would he send Fribble a postcard?

Fribble sat at the big library table in the reference section staring at the map of Italy for a long time. He'd learned where Italy was. But did that bring him any closer to discovering Mr. Crumb's new hobby? All he knew for sure was that Italy was in Europe, it was shaped like a boot, and it was a long way from Cheddarville.

Fribble climbed off the chair and went to tell Miss Scurry that he was finished looking at the atlas. She came and carefully carried the heavy book back to the shelf, and Fribble and Scamper walked home again.

Fribble had plenty to think about all afternoon: bugs, crabs, shrimps, gooey macaroni, and Italy. But puzzle over it as hard as he might, Fribble felt he was no closer to solving the mystery. He finally did his math homework, which was easy. He played a computer game, which was fun. And he thought more about the mystery, which was confusing.

After dinner, Fribble and his family sat around the television watching the news. They watched a piece about local amateur weather stations. The past summer, Wisconsin had had lots of tornadoes. The newscaster talked about a network of weather stations that was forming. He showed a picture of one home weather station with a complicated-looking tower on the roof. The newscaster went on to say that you could buy computer software and connect your personal station to the Weather Network Web site. If they used your weather data on television, you would be given credit and your name would be shown on the screen.

"That looks like fun," Fribble said. "You could help report the weather and your name would be on TV."

"You think any way to use the computer is fun," his mother observed. "You'd make your bed every morning by using the computer if you could. But those weather stations do sound useful. With more information coming in from all over the state, I'm sure they'll get better warnings about tornadoes and other storms."

After the news, Fribble's father switched off the television, and Fribble and Scamper read their library books again until it was time for bed.

Monday morning when Fribble and Scamper set off for school, Fribble glanced across the street to see if perhaps Mr. Crumb was already out working in his garden. Sometimes he got an early start to beat the heat. But he wasn't there today. Fribble wondered if he was inside reading library books or practicing Italian cooking.

Then Fribble happened to glance up, and what he saw made him stop dead in his tracks. He actually rubbed his paw across his eyes because he thought he must be seeing things. But no. Nothing was wrong with his eyes. There was Mr. Crumb, big as life, standing up on the roof of his house!

"Look!" Fribble whispered to Scamper, pointing up at Mr. Crumb.

"What's he doing up there?" Scamper asked.

"Don't ask me," Fribble said.

"Does it have something to do with his new hobby?"

"Maybe," Fribble said. He wanted to yell up to Mr. Crumb, but he didn't dare. Fribble was afraid a sudden shout might startle his old friend and maybe make him fall. It looked dangerous to be up so high. And Mr. Crumb wasn't just standing there. He seemed to be building something on top of his roof. There were long metal pieces. Fribble's mind flashed back to the long skinny package marked "fragile." Were these the pieces that had been inside the package the postman delivered?

"Come on," Scamper said, tugging on his brother's paw. "We don't want to be late." He half-dragged Fribble down the street.

Fribble usually enjoyed school, but today he couldn't wait for it to end. The moment the bell rang and he was excused, Fribble was out of there. He scurried home as fast as his feet could carry him.

When he got near his house, Fribble started scanning rooftops. Sure enough there was some sort of tower standing on Mr. Crumb's house. What could it be? He stopped and stared. Could it be a weather station?! Maybe Mr. Crumb was building a tower on his roof just like they showed on TV last night. Maybe that was going to be his new hobby!

Fribble's heart raced, and his nose twitched. This time he felt sure that he was onto something. He was about to solve the mystery, at last.

When he got right in front of his house, he looked over in Mr. Crumb's yard. No sign of him. Fribble checked out the roof again. No sign of him there, either. Drat!

Fribble went inside his house and tried to remember everything he could about the weather station he'd seen on the news last night. What were the names of all those instruments he'd looked at? And how on earth would you spell them?

Then another idea hit. He knew the newspaper had weather news. He grabbed a sheet of paper and a pencil and ran back downstairs to find the newspaper. He looked at the box on page two where his mother always checked the weather. Carefully he printed the word "weather" onto his paper. He could enter this in the card catalog at school tomorrow, and he'd probably be able to find lots of weather books and the names of all those instruments.

Fribble tucked his sheet of paper in his backpack to be sure he wouldn't forget it in the morning. Then he went out in the front yard and played catch with Scamper. Every so often, Fribble looked over at Mr. Crumb's. There was no one in the garden and no one on the roof, either.

Tuesday was library day at school for Fribble's class. Miss Longwhiskers, the librarian, read them a good story. Then they had time to pick out books. Fribble went straight to a computer. He typed in the word "weather" and waited to see what would happen. Lots of titles of books appeared. One was called *Kid's Book on Weather.* Fribble checked the numbers after the title. It was in the good old 500s section again, 551.63. Fribble went to the nonfiction section and quickly found the book.

When he went to check out his book, Miss Longwhiskers asked, "Interested in weather, Fribble?"

"Yes," Fribble said. "There was a really good story on the television news last night about weather stations in Wisconsin. They're going to help predict tornadoes."

"Oh, I read an article all about that weather network in the local newspaper last weekend," Miss Longwhiskers said. "Maybe you'd like to read it."

"We don't get that newspaper," Fribble said.

"We keep two weeks of newspapers here in the library on the shelf," Miss Longwhiskers explained.

"And in the public library, they keep three months of the paper in the reference section. They can even help you find newspaper articles from long ago that have been copied on microfilm."

"I didn't know anyone kept old newspapers," Fribble said. "I thought they just got put out for recycling the next day."

"Let me show you where our newspapers are," Miss Longwhiskers said. "And I'll help you find that article from last Sunday."

Quickly Miss Longwhiskers pulled out the Sunday newspaper and found the article about the weather station network. Using the copier, she helped Fribble make a copy of the article to take home.

"Thanks, Miss Longwhiskers," Fribble said. He was sure that when he got home and had time to read the newspaper article and the weather book, he'd know enough to tell Mr. Crumb that he'd solved the mystery and knew all about his new hobby.

When he got home Tuesday, Fribble went to his room and pulled the weather book he had checked out of the school library from his backpack. He sat down and began to read it immediately. The book was filled with lots of information on how to make weather instruments and set up a home weather station.

The more Fribble read, the more complicated it seemed. Fribble studied the pictures and wrote down several words. Soon he had a list: rain gauge, barometer, hygrometer, and anemometer.

Fribble thought he'd have to look up all of these words in a dictionary, but he found a glossary at the back of the book. It had some of the hard words used in the book along with their definitions.

Fribble looked up his list of words in the glossary, and he studied the meanings carefully. He could see that a lot of different things went into making weather predictions.

Every once in a while, Fribble stopped reading and ran to the window to look over at Mr. Crumb's. Still no one was in the yard or on the roof. Fribble studied the tower sticking up on Mr. Crumb's roof. It didn't look exactly like the one in the weather book, but then it was high and it was hard to see the details.

Next, Fribble began studying the article that had been in last Sunday's newspaper. It talked about the weather network and said you could call the local station, and they would send you a packet of free information.

Free anything appealed to Fribble so he decided this was a really good idea. He went down to the kitchen to show his mother the piece from the newspaper and ask if he could call the TV station.

"Yes, you may," his mother said. "Does it give the phone number?"

"No," Fribble said. He read out loud, "Call WMTV for a packet of free information."

"Well," his mother said. "I guess you'll have to look it up."

"In the library?" Fribble asked.

"The library has phone books for some cities, but you can use ours," his mother said. She got the phone book down from a shelf and handed it to Fribble. "Do you know how to find the number?"

"Is it like a dictionary?" Fribble asked.

"Sort of," his mother said. "It's arranged by the letters of the alphabet like a dictionary, but the telephone book has white pages, gray pages, blue pages, and yellow pages. The white pages have the phone numbers and addresses of houses listed by the people's last names. The gray pages have businesses listed by the names of the businesses. Blue pages give government information. And yellow pages are like ads, organized by groups like auto dealers and television stations."

"So I'd use the yellow pages, right?" Fribble said. "I'd look in the yellow pages in the 'T's' for TV stations."

"Right," his mother replied. While Fribble turned pages, his mother stood by, ready to help. But Fribble wanted to do it on his own. When he found the pages listing the addresses and phone numbers of "television stations," he looked for WMTV.

Fribble got a piece of paper and a pencil and wrote down the phone number.

Then he punched in the numbers, and someone answered the phone at the TV station. Fribble explained what he'd read in the paper and what hc wanted. The person at the TV station said she would send the packet right away.

Fribble went back to his room and started reading again.

Scamper came in. "Did you get another library book?" he asked, seeing the book that was open on Fribble's desk.

"Yeah."

"Can I look at it?" Scamper asked. "Does it have good pictures?"

"Sure, you can look," Fribble said. "Remember that program we saw on television about weather stations? Well, this book has pictures of lots of weather instruments that you can make."

"Cool," Scamper said. "Are we going to make a weather station, Fribble?"

"No, but I was wondering if that's what Mr. Crumb might be doing."

"Why don't we go ask him?" Scamper suggested. "I just saw him go out in his garden to work."

"Really!" Fribble said. He ran to the window and looked out. Sure enough, there was Mr. Crumb kneeling in his rose garden.

Fribble picked up the weather book and went outside with Scamper. Taking his little brother's paw and looking carefully to the right and the left, they walked across the street.

"Hi, Mr. Crumb," Fribble called. He was very excited at the prospect of telling his friend that he had finally discovered his secret.

"Hi there, Fribble and Scamper," Mr. Crumb said. "Oh, ho, I see you're carrying another book. What's this one about?"

"It's about *weather*," Fribble said, pausing just a moment before saying the last word in his sentence. He watched Mr. Crumb for some telltale sign, but Mr. Crumb seemed more interested in pulling out the grass that was creeping into his rose garden than he was in the weather.

"We watched a program on TV about tornadoes and home weather stations. Did you see it?"

"No," Mr. Crumb said. "I haven't watched much television lately. I've been busy reading my book."

"Too bad you missed that program," Fribble said. "I mean, it could have helped you a lot."

"Helped me?" Mr. Crumb said. "How would it have helped me?"

"It would have shown you how to put up a weather station," Fribble explained.

"But I'm not putting up a weather station," Mr. Crumb said.

"Isn't that going to be your new hobby?" Fribble asked. He felt a little uneasy. Could he be wrong again? "Aren't you going to use weather instruments to help forecast tornadoes and everything?"

For a moment Mr. Crumb looked very puzzled. Then a smile broke out on his face. "Oh," he said, "you must have noticed me up on my roof."

"Yeah, we did," Scamper said. "You were way up high, building something."

"I was indeed," Mr. Crumb said. "But I wasn't building a weather station."

"You weren't?" Fribble said. His whiskers drooped.

"No," Mr. Crumb said.

"You aren't going to put up an anemometer and a barometer and a hygrometer and a rain gauge?" Fribble demanded, using every one of the new weather words he'd just learned.

"No, I'm not," Mr. Crumb said.

"Then what *are* you building on your roof?"

"Ah, that's part of my secret," Mr. Crumb said. "Remember that I told you my new hobby was going to be a secret until I learned to do it well, and then I'd show you how?"

"Yeah, I remember," Fribble said.

He sighed as he put the weather book on the porch steps. Scamper sat beside it and started looking at the pictures again.

Fribble knelt down to help Mr. Crumb pull clumps of grass. And as he pulled, he thought. What could Mr. Crumb's secret be? Did the new hobby have something to do with gooey macaroni and Italian cooking? He certainly wasn't keeping insects or raising crabs or shrimps. And apparently Mr. Crumb wasn't going to be part of a weather station network, either. So what was that strange thing up on his roof? And what did it have to do with Mr. Crumb's new hobby?

Fribble fretted that evening because he had again failed to discover Mr. Crumb's new hobby. But the next morning he quickly forgot his disappointment when his teacher, Miss Niblett, wrote "Slipper, snack time, SSS" on the chalkboard. As usual, Fribble's curiosity kicked into high gear, and he wondered what the SSS would be.

Just before two o'clock, as promised, Slipper's mother arrived at school with treats for the class. "Since it's been so hot this September, I thought I'd cool us off with snowball snacks," Slipper announced. "Sweet September Snowballs. SSS. We made them last night." And she passed around a plate of miniature snowballs to everyone in the class. "They're made of cream cheese and sugar rolled in coconut," she explained.

The class grew quiet as each of them munched away on a little paw-sized snowball. Delicious! Fribble thought, as he ate.

Now that both his curiosity and hunger were satisfied, his mind was free to concentrate on Mr. Crumb's secret again. Since the new hobby didn't seem to have anything to do with insects or crabs or weather stations, Fribble went back to thinking about gooey macaroni, cooking, and traveling in Italy.

That afternoon, when Fribble went over to join Mr. Crumb in his garden, he was eager and ready to try to learn more about the mystery.

"Hi, there, Fribble," Mr. Crumb said. "Still enjoying your library books about insects and crustaceans and weather stations?"

"Yeah," Fribble said. "How are you doing on *your* book?" Fribble had noticed that the fat library book was back on the arm of the big wooden chair that Mr. Crumb always sat in on his front porch.

"Still reading it, and I'm studying another book, too."

"For your new hobby?" Fribble asked.

"Uh-huh," Mr. Crumb said with a smile.

Fribble waited, hoping that Mr. Crumb might volunteer a few more clues. But he kept weeding the flower bed and said nothing more at all. They worked quietly together for a while, and then Fribble started asking questions. "Do you like to travel?"

"Yes, I do," Mr. Crumb said.

"Ever been to Italy?" Fribble asked.

"No, I haven't," Mr. Crumb said.

"It's in Europe," Fribble said, proud to share his new knowledge.

"It's certainly a country I'd like to visit some day," Mr. Crumb said.

"I guess if you went there, you'd eat lots of *macaroni*," Fribble said.

"Probably," Mr. Crumb agreed. He turned and looked at his little friend. "Are you hungry, Fribble? I should have asked if you wanted an after-school snack."

"No, thank you, but I *am* thirsty," Fribble said. He'd been waiting for this chance. If Mr. Crumb went inside to get drinks, maybe Fribble could copy down the name of Mr. Crumb's book without being observed.

"Let's take a break from weeding, then," Mr. Crumb suggested.

They gathered up their tools and the bucket of weeds and went to the shady porch. The minute Mr. Crumb stepped inside to get some lemonade, Fribble pulled out the piece of paper and stubby pencil he'd tucked in his pocket and quickly copied down the name of the book Mr. Crumb was reading. It was a long and complicated name. Fribble shoved the paper and pencil back in his pocket and took a quick peek inside the book. Maybe he'd find a clue there.

There were few pictures in the heavy book and lots of words that Fribble didn't know. He put the book down on the arm of the chair before Mr. Crumb came back out with two glasses of lemonade.

Fribble tasted the cool drink. It was delicious. But he didn't have time today to lounge back and relax the way he usually did. Instead he drank quickly, far too excited to simply sit there on the porch and rest. He had an important clue in his back pocket. Once he studied it, he might be a lot closer to finding out what Mr. Crumb's secret was.

As soon as Fribble finished his lemonade, he hurried home and went straight to his room. He sat at his desk and spread out the piece of paper with the title to Mr. Crumb's book. It looked something like "Gooey Macaroni," but not quite. Fribble couldn't read it. He'd have to go to the school library tomorrow and see what he could find out. He slipped the piece of paper into his backpack so he'd be sure to remember it.

The next morning, Fribble left his brother at the kindergarten playground, and instead of going off to play, he went inside to the library. Miss Longwhiskers was working behind the counter. She always let students come in before school to return or check out books, but she didn't let them come in just to talk and visit.

Fribble went straight to a computer and began to use the catalog. After choosing "name," Fribble slowly and carefully typed in the two words on his slip of paper, "G u g l i e l m o M a r c o n i." Four books came up.

Fribble looked at these four book titles and noticed that they were all in 631.384. One was listed as part of the Giants of Science series. That sounded really important. Off Fribble went to the 600s section of nonfiction books. He found one of the books that was called *Guglielmo Marconi: Radio Pioneer.*

Fribble opened the book and found a picture of a man. His heart began beating fast. Marconi wasn't a gooey macaroni dish. He was an important man, a giant of science! Fribble took the book over to a table and began to read. He soon learned that Marconi was famous for his work with radio.

"Found a good book, Fribble?" asked Miss Longwhiskers, as she came over to see what he was reading.

"Yes, ma'am," Fribble said. "It's a book about a man called Macaroni."

"I think you mean Marconi, Fribble," Miss Longwhiskers said. "He's a very important man in the history of radio. You've already found a good book. If you want to know more about him, you can look him up in an encyclopedia."

"How do I do that?" Fribble asked.

Miss Longwhiskers took him to the reference section of the library and showed him several sets of encyclopedias. "This would be a good set for you to use," she suggested, pointing out a set with dark blue covers. She put her finger on the spine of the book. "See these letters? They tell you which topics are covered in which book. We want to find M a r c o n i. So where would we look?"

"Gee, there are two books starting with 'M,'" Fribble said, as he knelt down next to the set of books. "Which one should we use?"

"Volume 14 covers topics from 'Lighting to Maximilian,' and Volume 15 covers from 'Maximinus to Naples.' Look at the third letter in Marconi's name. Does 'Mar' come before or after 'Max'?" Miss Longwhiskers asked.

Fribble thought for a moment and silently ran through his ABC's. "'R' comes before 'X,'" he finally said, "so I think Marconi would be in Volume 14."

"You're right," Miss Longwhiskers said, smiling. "Now look and see." She helped Fribble find the entry for 'Marconi,' then Fribble sat down to read what it said about a young man who experimented with radios, sending aerials up high on kites and balloons. Fribble's eyes shone as he read how Marconi had gone on to win all kinds of prizes and medals.

After he finished reading the article in the encyclopedia, Fribble opened his book again. Right away he saw a picture of a radio antenna. Then it clicked! Mr. Crumb wasn't interested in the "feelers" of insects, and he wasn't building a weather tower on his roof. He was putting up a radio antenna!

Fribble wanted to run right home and tell Mr. Crumb what he'd learned. But just then, the first bell rang, and Fribble hurried to check out his book and rush to class. His discovery would have to wait until after school.

Fribble's long tail switched about wildly, and his whiskers quivered as he hurried down the hall to his second grade classroom. This time he had uncovered Mr. Crumb's secret. He was sure of it. His nose began to twitch. Fribble wanted nothing more than to rush to Mr. Crumb's house and tell him. But between Fribble and that goal was a very long day of school.

When the last bell finally rang that afternoon, Fribble scurried homeward. Anxiously he looked in his neighbor's yard, but there was no sign of Mr. Crumb. Fribble stopped in his house only long enough to drop his backpack and tell his mother that he was going across the street.

But as Fribble went charging down the steps of his front porch, he saw to his dismay that Mr. Crumb still wasn't out working in the garden. Drat! Fribble thought, stopping in his tracks. Where is he? Fribble stared at the yard across the street willing Mr. Crumb to appear.

He heard the door slam behind him, and Scamper ran up. "Want to play catch?" he asked hopefully.

"Not now," Fribble said. "I need to talk with Mr. Crumb."

"You'll have to yell, then," Scamper said.

"Why?" asked Fribble, turning to look at his little brother.

"Cause he's up on his roof again," Scamper pointed. "See?" Sure enough, Mr. Crumb was out on the roof of the old, Victorian two-story house.

Looking quickly to the right and left, Fribble took his little brother's paw and they dashed across the street. Mr. Crumb called and waved to them. "I'll be down in about ten minutes."

Fribble and Scamper sat on the grass where they could watch Mr. Crumb. Finally, they saw him gather up his tools and climb in through a window into the house. A few minutes later, he came out on the porch, bringing them all glasses of lemonade.

"Hello, there," he said, settling into his favorite chair as Fribble and Scamper joined him. "How about a cool drink? It's hot today working up on the roof."

Fribble took the glass offered to him, but he didn't drink. Instead, he set it on the table, and the words came rushing out of him. "I know what your secret is," he said. "I know what your new hobby is going to be!"

"Do you?" asked Mr. Crumb with a smile. "And what do you think it is?"

"You're building a really tall radio antenna, aren't you?" Fribble asked, jumping out of his chair to stand in front of Mr. Crumb, his tail lashing wildly in the air. "Your antenna is going to be *so* tall you'll be able to hear radio stations as far away as Italy, won't you? You'll be able to listen to music and sports and news broadcasts and everything, huh? That's going to be your new hobby. Listening to the radio!"

Mr. Crumb smiled. "Yes, I *am* building a radio antenna, Fribble. Good for you. You've figured out part of my secret. But I'm not building that antenna

just so I can listen to music. You're awfully close, but listening to radio programs is not going to be my new hobby."

"It isn't?" Fribble said. His whiskers drooped. He had been so sure that he had discovered Mr. Crumb's secret. Wrong again. He plopped down in a chair and began to sip his lemonade while he thought long and hard about this.

Mr. Crumb's hobby had something to do with radio. If it wasn't just *listening* to the radio, what was it? Was he going to listen to music until he was an expert and maybe become a disc jockey at a radio station? Fribble stared at Mr. Crumb. Somehow he couldn't picture his old friend as a disc jockey.

Could it be that he was going to specialize in building antennas? Maybe Mr. Crumb was going to get a little van and drive all around town putting up radio antennas for people? Could that be it? Fribble frowned. He didn't think so. That sounded more like a full-time job than a hobby. What was Mr. Crumb's secret? It was driving Fribble crazy.

"Are you finished building your antenna yet?" Fribble asked.

"No, it's not quite finished yet. I still have a little left to do."

"Could I help?" Fribble asked. He was sure it would help him get over his disappointment if he could run on the roof.

"Oh, I don't think your mother would like you climbing around on my roof," Mr. Crumb said. "You'll have to be patient a while longer. It's almost finished. But first I'm going to enjoy this cool drink."

Fribble sat back down and began sipping his lemonade, too.

"How did you figure it out, Fribble?" Mr. Crumb asked. "What made you decide that instead of keeping insects or building a weather station on my roof, I was building a radio antenna?"

"I noticed the name of the book you were reading," Fribble said. "And I looked up Marconi in the library. I read about him in the encyclopedia, and I checked out a book about him, too."

"You're getting to be a good researcher," Mr. Crumb said. "You've been spending a lot of time in the library."

Scamper, who never sat still for very long, jumped down from the porch and ran out on the lawn to look up at the antenna again.

"Your antenna's awfully tall," he pointed out.

Fribble set down his empty lemonade glass and went out to join his little brother. He gazed up at the antenna that reached high into the sky. "I'll bet it's the tallest thing on our block," he said.

"Maybe it's the tallest thing in the whole wide world!" Scamper added.

"No, it isn't," Fribble said. He turned and smiled at Mr. Crumb. How much higher was this antenna going to be? Was Mr. Crumb's secret that he was going to build the tallest radio antenna in all of Cheddarville? Could he do it?

"There are lots of tall buildings in the world," Fribble told his brother, "taller than anything in Cheddarville! And lots of tall antennas, too, I'll bet."

"You think you know so much! Can you prove it?" Scamper asked. "Are we going to the library to look for a book about the biggest and the tallest?"

"Why not?" asked Fribble. Since he couldn't help Mr. Crumb on the roof, and it was hard to just sit around and wait while the antenna got higher and higher, a trip to the library sounded good. It would be fun to go check out some books.

A few minutes later, Fribble and Scamper climbed the steps to the library again.

Miss Scurry smiled when they approached her desk and asked, "What are you two interested in today?"

"We want to know about the tallest and the biggest," Scamper said.

Miss Scurry looked puzzled.

Fribble asked, "Is there a book that would tell us what the highest radio antenna in the whole wide world is?"

"My goodness," Miss Scurry said. "You always have such fascinating questions. Yes, there is a book about the biggest and the tallest. It's called *Guinness World Records*. Let me get it for you."

Fribble and Scamper sat in the reference section again. "Let's see," Miss Scurry said. She turned to the table of contents, "Here's a section on 'Small Stuff,' that won't help. Ah, 'Technology,' that sounds promising." She ran her finger down the listings to "Buildings and Structures." She pointed out a paragraph to Fribble. "Here you are."

Miss Scurry left, and Fribble read to Scamper, "It says the tallest structure ever built was a radio mast in Poland. It was 2,120 feet and 8 inches tall."

"Wow! Guess that is higher than Mr. Crumb's roof, isn't it?" Scamper asked.

"Sure is. Oodles and oodles of times higher," Fribble said. "What a neat book!" And the two spent the next half hour reading fascinating facts. But, as interesting as this book was, Fribble's mind kept wandering back to Mr. Crumb's secret. What was Mr. Crumb going to do with his radio antenna?

Miss Scurry, the librarian, came back to the table where Fribble and Scamper still sat, reading fascinating information from *Guinness World Records*. "Anything else I can help you with?" she asked.

Hearing Miss Scurry's voice reminded Fribble that although he was having fun, he wasn't getting any closer to discovering Mr. Crumb's secret. Fribble closed the book. He furrowed his brow and stroked his whiskers thoughtfully. "I've *got* to learn more about radio. I'm missing something. What else do people do with radios besides just listening to music and news? I've already read in the encyclopedia about Marconi, and I've got a book about him, too. Where else could I look to learn more?"

"There's a lot to learn about radio," Miss Scurry said. "Antennas, sun spots, broadcasting, licenses, clubs, and all kinds of equipment. And there are lots of places where you can find information. Some of it is very complicated. But some of it isn't. My nephew, who's in middle school, made a crystal radio out of a kit. He keeps it in his bedroom and listens to music on it. And he says it wasn't hard to make at all."

"Really?" Fribble said. His shoulders, which had been sagging suddenly, straightened up. A gleam appeared in his eye. He pulled his little notebook and stubby pencil out of his pocket. "Crystal radio? How do you spell that?" he asked. Miss Scurry helped him spell "crystal," then she returned to her desk to help someone else.

Fribble stared at the words. He turned to Scamper. "I wonder what a crystal radio is. I've never heard of one. Could it have anything to do with Mr. Crumb's secret?"

"I've heard of a crystal ball," Scamper volunteered.

"I'm not talking about a crystal ball," Fribble said.

But Scamper continued. "I watched a television program once. There was a fortune-teller. She looked into a crystal ball and she could see all kinds of things. Like what's going to happen in the future."

"Do you think Mr. Crumb is going to dress up in a robe and turban and try to tell people what's going to happen in their future?" Fribble asked. "Not likely! He's going to use that tall antenna he put up on his roof to do something with radio."

"Why not look up crystal radio in the library catalog?" Scamper asked, already climbing out of his library chair.

Fribble smiled at his little brother. Scamper often strayed off topic and he was an awful tagalong, but Fribble had to admit that sometimes the little guy did come up with good ideas.

Fribble led the way straight to a computer, called up the library catalog, and clicked on "word." Then, letter by letter, he carefully typed in "crystal radio" and waited for the list of books to come up.

To Fribble's surprise, no book titles appeared. He frowned. "I must have done something wrong," he said to Scamper. He tried again. Nothing.

Fribble went over to Miss Scurry and told her his problem. She joined him and Scamper at the computer.

She watched him go through all the steps again. "You've done everything right," she told him. "We just don't have any books on crystal radios."

"You don't?" Scamper's voice was filled with disbelief. "Haven't people written books about them?"

"I'm sure they have, but we can't buy every new book that comes out. We pick the books that we think most people want to read. And sometimes we don't have books on a good topic like crystal radios."

Fribble's whiskers drooped. The library had never failed him before.

"But I'm sure we can find you some information about crystal radios on the Internet," Miss Scurry continued.

Fribble perked up a little. "What's the Internet?" he asked.

"It's a great source of information. I'm going to show you how to use it," Miss Scurry said. "I think you're in for a big surprise."

Fribble snapped to attention. His nose began to twitch. A *surprise?* Whatever the Internet was, Fribble was already interested.

Miss Scurry led Fribble and Scamper to a computer that was connected to the Internet. "Lots of articles about all kinds of subjects are available on the Internet. To find them, you need to use a good search engine."

"What's a search engine?" Fribble asked.

"Is it like the little engine that thought it could?" asked Scamper.

Miss Scurry smiled. "Not really," she said. "But you know how a librarian can help you locate books and information in the library? A search engine is a computer tool that helps you find information on the Internet."

Miss Scurry showed Fribble which buttons to press and how to connect the library computer to the Internet. She showed him where to type in "crystal radio set." In just a few seconds, dozens of entries appeared.

"Wow!" Fribble said to Scamper. "Just look at that!"

Fribble read one entry after another in astonishment. You could make a crystal radio using

an oatmeal box, a wooden cigar box, or you could buy a kit. There were clubs you could join and contests you could enter. This was exciting! His whiskers twitched. Fribble looked at the drawings on the screen. It still looked pretty complicated to him. He wondered if, with Mr. Crumb's help, *he* could build a crystal radio.

While he was still staring at the screen, Miss Scurry checked in with them. "Oh, good," she said. "You've found a lot of information."

"But how will I ever remember all this stuff?" Fribble said.

"You can print it out using this printer," Miss Scurry explained. And within a few minutes, Fribble clutched a diagram of a crystal radio set tightly in his paws. He and Scamper hurried homeward. They went straight to Mr. Crumb's house.

"Look what I have," Fribble shouted, from halfway across the street. He ran up on Mr. Crumb's porch and spread out the directions for the crystal radio on the table.

"A crystal radio." Mr. Crumb smiled. "Hey, that's a great idea. You can listen to the news and music from the local radio station."

"Really?" said Fribble. "Does a crystal radio kit cost a lot of money?"

"No," Mr. Crumb said. "Less than ten dollars."

"Does it need an antenna like yours?" Scamper asked.

"It needs an antenna," Mr. Crumb said. "But not a tower like mine."

Fribble thought about that. If a crystal radio didn't need a tower, then it definitely wasn't going to be Mr. Crumb's hobby. Fribble had failed again to solve the mystery but he liked the idea of building his own radio. "Is it very hard to make a crystal radio?"

"Not really," Mr. Crumb said. "You could do it, and I'd be glad to supervise if you want. I can make suggestions if you get stuck, kind of like I did last year with your volcano science fair exhibit."

"Would you?" Fribble said. "I have some money saved up. Enough, I think. Would you help me get the kit?"

"Yes, indeed," Mr. Crumb replied. "I'll ask your mother and see if we can go shopping after school on Monday. Okay?"

"Great," Fribble said.

That night at dinner, all Fribble could talk about was the crystal radio set that he and Mr. Crumb were going to make. He was still talking about it the next morning at breakfast.

"Will I be able to listen to music on your radio, Fribble?" Scamper asked.

"'Course you will," Fribble said. But he worried just a little. He hadn't any idea how a crystal radio set worked. Would he really be able to build one? And although Fribble was thrilled with the idea of making his very own radio, he was discouraged that he still hadn't discovered Mr. Crumb's secret. What was Mr. Crumb up to? How could he find out?

Monday after school, Fribble needed no reminders
to hurry home—he knew he was going shopping
with Mr. Crumb. He ran into his house, dropped his
books, greeted his mother, picked up his money,
and raced across the street. Mr. Crumb was sitting in
his porch chair, thumbing through some magazines.

"I've been looking at different kinds of crystal
radio sets that are advertised in these magazines,"
Mr. Crumb explained. "We want to get the very
best buy for your money." He pointed to a picture
in the magazine. "Here's one that doesn't need any

batteries. The parts snap together. And it only has ten pieces. What do you think?"

Fribble said, "Looks good to me."

"Then let's go," said Mr. Crumb. They climbed into Mr. Crumb's old car, buckled up, and were on their way.

As they drove, Fribble tried to find ways to get Mr. Crumb to drop a clue about his secret. He casually asked questions on radio topics he'd seen recently on the Internet—sun spots, code tests, and of course, radio towers. But Mr. Crumb smiled, said little, and concentrated on his driving.

The clerk in the hobby store took the kit down from the shelf and made several cheerful comments about what fun they were going to have. It seemed that in no time at all, Fribble and Mr. Crumb were headed home again. Fribble proudly held the kit tightly between his paws in his lap. He only wished Mr. Crumb would drive faster. Fribble could hardly wait to begin to build his radio.

They parked the car and went inside to Mr. Crumb's kitchen table. Fribble opened the box. Inside was a plastic bag containing a red base, yellow tuning knob, and several small bags with other tiny pieces. There was also an instruction booklet.

Fribble opened the little bags and lined up all of the parts just like the picture in the booklet. Then he began at step one, putting in the spring connectors. Most of the pieces snapped in place. Mr. Crumb went off to get a Phillips screwdriver to put in the three small screws that held the tuning knob.

The most complicated piece was a little square box with two wires coming out of it. The booklet had a picture of this, and underneath it was labeled "capacitor." Just as the picture showed, Fribble bent the two wires out straight from the box.

"Oh!" Fribble suddenly gasped as one of the wires came off in his paws. Fribble looked first in his paw and then up at Mr. Crumb. His whiskers twitched. "I broke it," he said. "I thought I was being real careful, but I broke it."

"Not to worry," Mr. Crumb said. "I can fix it. Only take a minute." He led Fribble downstairs to his workshop and took out a soldering iron and plugged it in. He heated the wire and the metal strip coming from the little box until they were hot, and then touched them with the solder, which melted. When it was cool, they were joined together. "Good as new," Mr. Crumb said.

"Thanks, Mr. Crumb," Fribble said as they climbed the stairs from the basement back to the kitchen. "I'll be super, super careful this time. Promise."

And Fribble was extra careful in bending the wire and slipping it into place.

Finally, the crystal radio was all hooked up. Dangling from the set were the earphone, a long yellow wire, and a long red wire.

"The red one is the ground wire," Mr. Crumb explained. "You need to wrap the bare end of that wire around the water faucet here in the sink. The water faucet is attached to water pipes that go right down under the ground."

Fribble quickly took the red wire and gave it a few turns around the faucet.

"The yellow wire is your antenna," Mr. Crumb said. "You need to stretch it out as far as you can."

"How about taping it up the door of the broom closet?" Fribble asked.

"Perfect," Mr. Crumb said. He went and got a piece of tape and helped Fribble tape the antenna wire to the closet door.

"Now," Mr. Crumb said, placing the red plastic

stand on the kitchen sink, "put the earphone in your ear."

Fribble's paw trembled as he picked up the earphone and put it in his ear. He turned the yellow knob. Suddenly he heard music! Fribble's face lit up. "Listen!" he said, handing the earphone to Mr. Crumb.

Mr. Crumb listened, too. "Aha!" he said. "It works!"

They went around the house, attaching the wire to different pipes and stretching the antenna in different spots. In some places they could hardly hear the disc jockey and the music, but in other places it came in loud and clear.

Finally, Fribble neatly packed his radio back into the box and went home. Scamper was waiting for him. "Did you get it made, Fribble?" he asked.

"Sure did," Fribble replied.

"And can I listen?"

"Yes, indeed," Fribble said. "As soon as I set it up."

Fribble took the radio into the kitchen while Scamper danced around him. Fribble hooked up the ground wire onto the faucet. Then he took the antenna wire and tossed it over the door to the dining room. Finally, he placed the set on the table,

put in his earphone, and used the tuner. Once he heard music, he took the earphone and helped Scamper place it in his ear.

Fribble didn't have to ask if his brother could hear anything. Scamper's face lit up and his eyes grew big. "Ooooh," he said. "Music." And he tapped his foot.

Fribble looked thoughtful. He was proud of his crystal radio. But he still didn't know Mr. Crumb's secret. Why did Mr. Crumb need such a tall radio antenna?

That question was still in his mind the next day at school when he went to his library period. Fribble headed straight for the computer that was hooked up to the Internet. He typed in "radio antenna" and waited. Fribble read about several radios that were advertised in an *Amateur Radio Magazine,* and he saw announcements for "ham fests." Fribble wondered what they were. Festivals or picnics? What was their connection with radios? If they had anything to do with ham and cheese sandwiches, Fribble knew he'd like them. He thought ham was almost as good as gooey macaroni.

Then Fribble found a listing that said, "What is Ham Radio?" Fribble clicked on it and began to read about ham, or amateur, radio operators, their equipment, and their licenses. Aha! Fribble realized. Mr. Crumb was going to be a ham radio operator. That was his secret! He wasn't going to just listen to the radio. He was going to talk to people all over the world. Fribble's eyes glistened, and his heart beat fast! He'd discovered the secret. This time he was sure of it!

As he sat triumphant at the computer, Fribble still wanted to know more. He wanted to show off for Mr. Crumb. He knew he didn't have time to read a lot of books. Then he remembered the magazines that Mr. Crumb had been studying yesterday. Maybe some magazines would have information about ham radio.

Fribble slipped off the computer seat and went to find Miss Longwhiskers. He explained to her what he was looking for.

"This time, Fribble," she explained, "you need to use a special book that is a guide to what's been written in several popular magazines. It's called the *Reader's Guide to Periodical Literature*. I'll help you. We'll look up 'ham radio' in the subject guide, and it will give us a list of articles and the names of the magazines."

Fribble found only two radio magazines in the school library, but soon he was happily sitting at a library table reading them. He could hardly wait to see Mr. Crumb!

The moment library period ended, Fribble went down the hall to his classroom still clutching the magazines he'd just checked out. He went straight up to his teacher, Miss Niblett, and said, "I'd like to sign up for SSS time tomorrow afternoon, and I'd like to invite my neighbor, Mr. Crumb, to come to school."

"Ooooh," Miss Niblett said. "I'll bet you have something really special to share."

Fribble was glad she didn't ask any questions because that would spoil his surprise. She walked over to the chart that hung on the wall behind her desk and wrote in "Fribble" for the one o'clock SSS time on Wednesday. She gave Fribble a big wink before he scurried back to his desk.

As soon as he got home from school, Fribble hurried across the street. Mr. Crumb was sitting in his big chair.

"Ham radio!" Fribble shouted, without even waiting to say hello as he climbed the steps to the porch. "Your new hobby is ham radio, isn't it?"

Mr. Crumb smiled. "Good for you, Fribble. You should be very proud of yourself. You figured out my secret. Yes, I've been studying for an amateur radio license, and now I've got my radio station all hooked up. I'll show it to you if you like."

"Really?" Fribble's whiskers were aquiver. His heart was pounding in his chest. This time he was right! He'd discovered the secret at last! And Mr. Crumb was about to share it with him. "What are we waiting for?" Fribble shouted.

Mr. Crumb took him inside his house to a small room on the ground floor. In a corner of the room was a desk and on top of the desk was all kinds of interesting looking equipment.

Mr. Crumb sat at his desk and put on a set of earphones. Then he began to slowly twist some of the dials of the radio in front of him. Finally he took off the earphones and held them out to Fribble. "Put these on," he said.

Fribble stood next to Mr. Crumb and listened intently. "What is that?" he asked.

"Let me listen again, and I'll tell you," Mr. Crumb said. He put the earphones back on. "It's someone called Squeaker in the town of Edam," Mr. Crumb said. "He's using Morse code. Those short and long sounds you hear are called dots and dashes. They stand for letters of the alphabet."

"And you can hear those dots and dashes all the way from Edam?"

"Oh, you can hear a lot farther than that," Mr. Crumb said. "If we're lucky, some day you'll hear all the way to Italy! Now, let me see if I can find someone who's using voice instead of code." Once more he twisted the dials of the radio receiver.

Fribble was fascinated by the chirps, squeaks, and whistles that he heard. Suddenly, instead of dots and dashes, a voice came from the radio. It was a man calling, "CQ. CQ. This is N-zero-OUV calling CQ."

"Ham operators use letters and numbers that are referred to as call signs to identify themselves," Mr. Crumb explained. "The man we just heard has the call sign N-zero-OUV." Mr. Crumb picked up a small microphone and pushed his thumb down on a button. "N-zero-OUV this is KA-zero-YSK," Mr. Crumb said.

"Hello there, KA-zero-YSK," the voice answered. "I hear you loud and clear. This is Muncher here in Tillamook. How do you copy?"

"The name here is Crumb. I'm brand-new at this. I just got my station set up yesterday. I have here with me my young friend and neighbor, Fribble. He's just built a crystal radio. I wonder if you would mind saying hello to him. Back to you."

"I'd be glad to," said the voice. "Put him on."

Mr. Crumb handed the microphone to Fribble and said, "Go ahead. You push this button down to talk. When you're finished talking, release the button, and listen."

Fribble's tail switched through the air, and his eyes sparkled. He took the microphone. Carefully he pushed the button down and, using his deepest voice, said, "This is Fribble Mouse speaking. I'm in Cheddarville. Can you hear me?" He released the button.

"Yes, I can hear you, Fribble. My name is Muncher. I'm glad you're interested in radio. And I hope to hear from you again."

Fribble turned the microphone over to Mr. Crumb and waited as Mr. Crumb and Muncher talked for a short while. Then Mr. Crumb signed off using his call sign.

"Well, Fribble, what do you think? You've had your very first radio contact."

"It was fun," Fribble said. "When I'm older, I'll want you to teach me ham radio. But right now, I'm happy with my crystal radio set. And I want to show it to the kids in my class. Could you come to school tomorrow afternoon and help me set it up?"

"Sure could," Mr. Crumb said. "I'd be proud to."

After lunch at school the next day, Fribble kept his eyes on the classroom clock. The hands moved very slowly. Finally, just before one o'clock, Mr. Crumb arrived. Fribble almost didn't recognize him. Instead of wearing his old straw hat and gardening clothes, Mr. Crumb was dressed in his best dark blue suit. He smiled at Fribble when he came through the classroom door. Fribble jumped up and ran to introduce him to Miss Niblett.

Miss Niblett gathered the class in a circle on the carpet for sharing time. She pulled up a chair next to hers where Mr. Crumb sat. The chair was small and low so Mr. Crumb's knees stuck way up in the air. He held the box containing the crystal radio on his lap. When the class had settled down, Miss Niblett said, "Fribble has something special to share with us today."

Feeling very important, Fribble stood up and went to stand in front of the group. He was a little nervous at the thought of talking to everybody, but mostly he was excited. He smoothed out his whiskers.

"This is my neighbor, Mr. Crumb," Fribble said, smiling over at his friend. "He's taken up a new hobby. Amateur radio. He's what's called a ham radio operator. He put a big antenna on his roof, took lots of tests, and got a license. Now he can use his radio to talk to people all over the world. He lets me talk to people, too."

All eyes were on Mr. Crumb.

"I can't get a fancy radio like his, yet," Fribble continued. "But I learned that there are lots of other kinds of radios. And I built one all by myself." Then, remembering the broken wire, he added, "Of course, Mr. Crumb helped me a little. Mine is called a crystal radio set, and it really works!"

There was a little gasp from his classmates.

"Now I'm going to hook my radio up and show you." Mr. Crumb handed Fribble the box. Fribble

took out his radio and set it on the floor where the other students could see it.

Then Fribble took the red ground wire and wrapped it around the faucet in the classroom sink. He took the yellow antenna wire and Mr. Crumb helped him tape it high onto a nearby cupboard door.

Fribble came back to the circle and put the earphone in his ear. He was so excited, he was barely breathing, and he could hear his heart beating fast—almost like Morse code. Then faintly, he heard music from the local radio station. He turned the yellow dial until the music came in louder. Fribble broke into a big smile.

"I'll pass the earphone around and you can listen," Fribble said.

"And while we take turns listening," Miss Niblett said, "anyone can ask a radio question of Mr. Crumb or Fribble."

Mr. Crumb fielded lots of questions about radio tests and antennas as each member of the class took a turn listening to Fribble's crystal radio.

Then Tweek asked, "Who built the first radio?"

Instead of answering, Mr. Crumb looked at Fribble. Fribble said, "An inventor from Italy called Marconi made the first radio in 1895."

"Where's Italy?" asked Tweek.

Without hesitating, Fribble walked over to a map of Europe that was hanging on the classroom wall. It was easy to find the boot-shaped country. "Here's Italy," he said. Then he walked back to the sharing circle.

"Wow! How did you learn so much, Fribble?" asked Tweek.

"I've been spending a lot of time in the library reading all kinds of books and magazines," Fribble said.

Fribble smiled to himself. No point in telling them that I also learned a lot about insects, crabs, shrimps, and weather stations, he thought.

Fribble felt like a hero for the rest of the day. When the bell rang and he was gathering up his homework and heading out of school, students in his class kept coming up to him and asking questions or telling him how extra special they thought his radio was.

As soon as he got home, Fribble told Scamper and his mother all about his SSS afternoon. He set up the crystal radio again in the kitchen, and he and Scamper took turns listening to it.

Finally, Fribble put the radio away. He and Scamper took their ball and gloves and went out in the front yard to play catch.

It wasn't long before the mailman arrived. When Fribble noticed the mailman wasn't just putting letters into Mr. Crumb's mailbox, but was parking the truck in order to get a package out of the back, he stopped playing catch to turn and look.

Fribble and Scamper stared as the mailman walked up the steps onto the porch and rang Mr. Crumb's bell. This time the package that he handed over to Mr. Crumb wasn't long and narrow. It was small and square.

What could it be? Fribble wondered. Another secret? Fribble's whiskers quivered, and his long tail snapped through the air.